Adventures of the Little Green Dragon

Adventures of the Little Green Dragon

Mari Privette Ulmer

Illustrations by
Mary Kurnick Maass

UNITY® Books

Unity Village, Missouri

First Edition 1999

A Wee Wisdom® Book
for the child within us all

To receive a catalog of all our Unity publications (books, cassettes, compact discs, and magazines) or to place an order, call our Customer Service Department (816) 969-2069 or 1-800-669-0282.

The publisher wishes to acknowledge the editorial work of Michael Maday, Raymond Teague, Brenda Markle, Gayle Revelle, and Joanne Englehart; the copyediting and proof-reading of Kay Thomure, Thomas Lewin, Shari Behr, and Deborah Dribben; the production help of Rozanne Devine and Jane Blackwood; and the marketing efforts of Allen Liles and Sharon Sartin.

Cover design by Gretchen West

Library of Congress Cataloging-in-Publication Data

Ulmer, Mari Privette.
    Adventures of the Little Green Dragon / Mari Privette Ulmer ; illustrations by Mary Kurnick Maass. — 1st ed.
       p.   cm.
    Summary: In ten stories an ugly little green dragon finds self-acceptance and makes discoveries about how people should treat each other. Includes a brief guide for each story, identifying its lesson and providing discussion questions.
    ISBN 0-87159-228-2
    Canada BN 13252 9033 RT
    [1. Dragons—Fiction. 2. Self-acceptance—Fiction. 3. Conduct of life—Fiction.]
I. Maass, Mary Kurnick, ill. II. Title.
PZ7.U348Ad 1998
[E]—dc21
                                          98-41428
                                                 CIP
                                               AC

Unity Books feels a sacred trust to be a healing presence in the world. By printing with biodegradable soybean ink on recycled paper, we believe we are doing our part to be wise stewards of our Earth's resources.

Table of Contents

Foreword

Let's talk dragons, little green and otherwise.

First, what about those dragons? Are they good or bad? And why is Unity, an educational movement dedicated to helping people realize their oneness with God, publishing stories about a dragon?

Our thoughts are prayers, and our perceptions help create our world, according to Unity beliefs. That principle applies to dragons too. The answer to whether dragons are good or bad depends on one's perception of them. In Europe, and thus generally in North America as well, dragons traditionally have been viewed as evil beasts that mortals must conquer. In Asia, however, dragons have fared much better. Particularly in China and Japan, dragons have long been regarded as friendly harbingers of wealth and good luck. The dragon is considered far from evil in China. In fact, the dragon's image frightens away evil spirits—that's why the dragon is a regular feature in Chinese New Year's Day parades.

In recent years in the West, especially in literature and popular art, the Eastern view of dragons has come into vogue. Children's picture book authors and illustrators and artists of all sorts, including potters and painters, usually depict dragons, not as ferocious, fire-breathing lizards, but as adorable, personable, lovable creatures—like the Little Green Dragon.

Thus we amusingly identify with paintings of dragons eating chocolate chip cookies. We drink out of mugs with tiny dragons peering up at us with every sip. We hum along with dragon songs such as my personal favorite about the ever-frolicking magical dragon Puff. At Disney World we meet Figment, the little purple dragon of imagination. We are entertained by joyous dancing, singing, and talking dragons of various colors and sizes in movies and on television.

Now, some people may not choose to think about dragons at all, and that is their freewill choice. After all, reference books tell us that dragons are mythical beasts. But metaphysical folk and Joseph Campbell readers tend to find much symbolism and Truth in traditional myths. Hailing from imaginary realms and being highly individualistic, dragons in literature and art can mirror certain attributes of humans and reflect qualities humans wish that they claimed more of as their own. In short, they can be images that help teach us lessons about ourselves—like our Little Green Dragon.

Unity Books, then, declares that the Little Green Dragon is good and is a helpful teacher—even beneficial in assisting children of all ages to remember their own Christ nature and innate Godliness. Our Little Green Dragon is a kind, friendly, brave, loving guide who can spur children to become aware of their own sense of self-worth as well as bolster their own self-esteem.

As poet Marianne Moore exclaims:

> *O to be a dragon,*
> *a symbol of the power of Heaven*

Secondly, how did the Little Green Dragon come to literary life and to Unity? To answer these questions, we must turn first to Mari Privette Ulmer.

The author of the Little Green Dragon's adventures has been telling stories since the age of five and under orders from her mother to keep neighborhood children peaceful. She was too small to keep the peace forcefully, so she told stories to quiet the children. As an adult, Mari never lost her love of storytelling; before entering law school and becoming an attorney, she was the "Story Lady" for a Kansas City television station during the early 1960s.

While doing these TV broadcasts, the Little Green Dragon hatched out of Mari's imagination and her own childhood feelings. Mari was first introduced to Unity when in 1969 it was recommended that she submit her stories to *Wee Wisdom*, Unity's children's magazine started by Myrtle Fillmore. Mari actually submitted not a manuscript but a tape recording of herself telling the story of the Little Green Dragon.

Wee Wisdom editor Tom Hopper liked the stories, and they ran as a series from March 1969 to November 1972. Readers quickly agreed with Hopper's taste in dragons. In 1971 Unity School published the first seven stories as a promotional booklet for renewing subscribers (80,000 were published). At that time Mari recorded an audiocassette of the dragon stories for Unity, and the booklet was sent free to all who ordered the tape.

The oral tradition in literature is probably as old as dragon myths, and the Little Green Dragon adventures fit snugly in that genre. The stories are perfect for reading aloud. Children especially enjoy their repetition and playfulness. "They are told stories, not written stories," Mari said, adding that she "wrote" them by reciting them aloud.

Early studies and interviews with parents, educators, and children confirmed the author's estimation of the Little Green Dragon stories as worthy building blocks for children's self-esteem in primary grades. "Through the adventures of this little creature, a child learns life lessons about love, courage, and identity," Mari said. "The Little Green Dragon speaks to children of every background and ethnicity."

Unity minister Alden Studebaker and his wife Donna, a licensed Unity teacher, agree with Mari about the value of the stories. Several years ago they urged Unity Books editor Michael Maday to consider republishing the Little Green Dragon stories. Donna

Studebaker grew up reading the stories herself, read them to children with whom she babysat, and then read them to her own three children.

"I've always loved mythology and fantasy stories," said Donna Studebaker. "What I like now is that the Little Green Dragon is accepted for what he is. He comes so much from love.… He is so caring. There is a real gentleness about the stories.… He gets into trouble, but it turns out all right."

With Michael's blessings, first associate editor Gayle Revelle and then Brenda Markle enthusiastically began working to give the Little Green Dragon a new life. With a longtime affinity for all creatures fanciful and dragonish, I happily inherited the project from my predecessors.

This new edition of the beloved Little Green Dragon stories involves some changes. Even little green dragons mature a bit over time. Those who remember the Little Green Dragon from *Wee Wisdom* will note immediately that he looks much different. The illustrations for the magazine were by Gordon Laite, the son of famous illustrator Kate Greenaway. Laite's Little Green Dragon resembles an insect. Artist Mary Kurnick Maass has given us a wonderful, new, softer and gentler dragon, decidedly more cute than ugly. The use of repetition in the stories has been expanded, but adjusted somewhat to fit the sensibilities of modern readers and the Little Green Dragon's new look.

The Little Green Dragon retains all of his original charm, however. It is our hope at Unity Books that children and their young-at-heart guardians and educators will enjoy discovering and rediscovering these ten original adventures. The book concludes with a short guide to identify some important lessons in the stories and to spark discussion with children.

May all readers derive big dragon-size pleasure from the Little Green Dragon's adventures.

—Raymond Teague
May 1998

Raymond Teague is associate editor of Unity Books and has been children's book editor of the *Fort Worth Star-Telegram* for twenty years. He has written articles and spoken extensively about children's books.

Little Green Dragon Meets the Princess

ONCE upon a long-ago morning, the Little Green Dragon woke up.

First, he opened his big green eyes.

Next, he decided to go visit the princess. He loved the princess, because she was *so-o-o-o-o pretty*!

In a little while the Little Green Dragon was walking along the road. He was on his way to visit the princess.

The Little Green Dragon saw a man on a horse galloping toward him.

"Hi!" the Little Green Dragon called out.

But ... when the man and the horse saw the Little Green Dragon, they *fainted*. They thought he was *so-o-o-o-o ugly*!

Sadly, the Little Green Dragon went walking on his way to see the princess.

Soon he came to a town.

All the people were running about and crying: "Whatever shall we do? Whatever shall we do? The wicked king and all his army are coming to make war on the princess!"

The Little Green Dragon went running from one group of people to another.

He said: "I'll help! I'll help fight the wicked king and all his army."

But ... when the people of the town saw the Little Green Dragon, they *fainted*—this way and that way, and that way and this way. They thought he was *so-o-o-o-o ugly*!

1

"Just wanted to help," the Little Green Dragon said softly.

Very sadly, the Little Green Dragon went on his way to see the princess.

After a long while he came to a mountain. At the very top was a castle where the princess lived.

The Little Green Dragon climbed. He climbed and climbed and climbed. He climbed to the top of the mountain.

The castle was in front of him.

The Little Green Dragon walked across the castle bridge into the castle courtyard.

All the soldiers were running about. They were crying: "Whatever shall we do? Whatever shall we do? The wicked king and all his army are coming to make war on the princess!"

The Little Green Dragon went walking very quietly past the soldiers. Luckily, none of them saw him, so none of them fainted.

The Little Green Dragon went inside the castle to see the princess. He loved the princess because she was *so-o-o-o-o pretty*!

Peering down one long hall after another, the Little Green Dragon looked for the princess.

Then ... he saw her coming toward him!

But ... when the princess saw the Little Green Dragon, she *fainted*! She too thought he was *so-o-o-o-o ugly*!

"I just wanted to tell her I would help. I love her," the Little Green Dragon said softly.

Very, very sadly, the Little Green Dragon walked out of the castle, through the castle courtyard, and across the castle bridge.

He walked down the other side of the mountain. Maybe the people there would not think he was *so-o-o-o-o ugly*.

As the Little Green Dragon walked, big green tears dripped off the end of his long green nose.

He didn't look anywhere but at the ground. He was very, very, very sad.

Then the Little Green Dragon heard a terrible racket. He looked up.

There, right in front of him, were the wicked king's lancers and bow-men, his horsemen, and his foot soldiers—and the wicked king himself!

Ever so bravely, the Little Green Dragon went running toward the wicked king.

He was crying: "Please don't make war on the princess! Please don't!"

But ... when the lancers and bowmen, the horsemen and foot soldiers, and the wicked king himself saw the Little Green Dragon, they *fainted*. Yes, they thought he was *so-o-o-o-o ugly*!

Then the Little Green Dragon heard another terrible racket. Slowly, slowly, he turned his head and peered over his shoulder.

There, behind him, were the man and the horse who had fainted, the people of the town who had fainted, the soldiers of the princess who hadn't fainted because they hadn't seen him ... and the princess herself!

4

They were all yelling and shouting and cheering.

The Little Green Dragon was frightened, because they were looking straight at him. Nobody had ever looked straight at him before—without fainting, that is.

Then ... the princess herself came running to the Little Green Dragon.

She threw her arms around his rough, green neck and said: "Oh, Little Green Dragon. You saved us from the wicked king and all his army! And, oh, how we love you, because you are exactly who you are."

And then the princess laughed and said, "And because you are *so-o-o-o-o special.*"

Little Green Dragon Meets Big Dragon

ONCE upon a long-ago morning, the Little Green Dragon woke up.

First, he opened his big green eyes. Then he uncurled his long green tail from around his little green self.

Little Green Dragon had been dreaming of the princess. He loved the princess *so-o-o-o-o much.*

Because it was spring, the Little Green Dragon decided he would go away for a while.

The Little Green Dragon took off his little green nightcap with the l-o-n-n-g tassel. He put on his little green daycap with the feather that curled.

Then the Little Green Dragon went walking, walking, walking down the other side of the mountain.

The Little Green Dragon hadn't gone very far when … what do you think? A mountain lion jumped out from behind a boulder! But the mountain lion didn't roar. He said, "SH-H-H-H-H!"

"Why do you say sh-h-h-h-h?" asked the Little Green Dragon.

"Because," said the lion, "the dragon might hear you!"

"But *I am* the dragon!" said Little Green Dragon.

The lion began to laugh. The lion hee-hee-ed and ho-ho-ed and ha-ha-ed. He covered his mouth with his paws so he wouldn't make any noise. And he snorted and carried on.

The Little Green Dragon kept saying, "Please, sir ..."

But the lion just kept on hee-hee-ing and ho-ho-ing and ha-ha-ing. So finally, Little Green Dragon went on his way down the mountainside.

"But *I am* the dragon," he muttered to himself.

"SH-H-H!" said a voice. Little Green Dragon looked up. He saw a woman all hunkered down. She was quietly patting seeds into the ground with her hands.

"Hi!" said Little Green Dragon.

"SH-H-H!" said the woman.

"Why do you tell me to sh-h-h?" asked Little Green Dragon.

"SH-H-H-H-H!" said the woman.

Little Green Dragon whispered, "Why do you tell me to sh-h-h-h-h?"

"Because the dragon will hear you," whispered the woman.

"But *I am* the dragon," whispered Little Green Dragon back to her.

The woman began to laugh. She chuckled and chortled. She put her hands over her mouth to try to muffle the noise. She snorted and carried on. "Madame, please," said Little Green Dragon. The woman went on laughing. "Why is it that everyone laughs when I say that *I am* the dragon?"

The woman took one hand away from her mouth long enough to point. "You?" she chuckled and chortled. "You?" and she fell down backwards. She covered her head with her arms. She laughed and she laughed.

Little Green Dragon walked on down the mountain muttering, "But *I am* the dragon ... *I am* the dragon."

8

As he walked, he noticed there was no grass and no trees. The ground looked all funny. It was black and brown. The rocks looked smudgy. In fact, the whole side of the mountain looked as if it had been burned. Little Green Dragon stopped. He looked and he looked.

Then he listened and he listened. But he didn't hear a sound—not one sound. No birds twittered. No bugs or bees buzzed. Everything was quiet as could be. You know, it was kind of scary!

At the bottom of the mountain was the town. Little Green Dragon didn't see any people in the town.

At the top of the mountain, looking down on the town, was the castle of the princess. Little Green Dragon didn't see any soldiers or footmen or knights or ladies at the castle.

And Little Green Dragon didn't hear a single sound.

Little Green Dragon went walking, walking, walking along the ribbledy, wobbledy cobblestones of the town. All the doors were shut. All the shutters were shut on the windows. No dogs barked. No cats meowed. No horses clippety-clopped. And no people made any people noises.

Little Green Dragon looked all around with his big green eyes.

He took a big, deep breath. He called out in his loudest voice: "HI! ANYBODY HOME?"

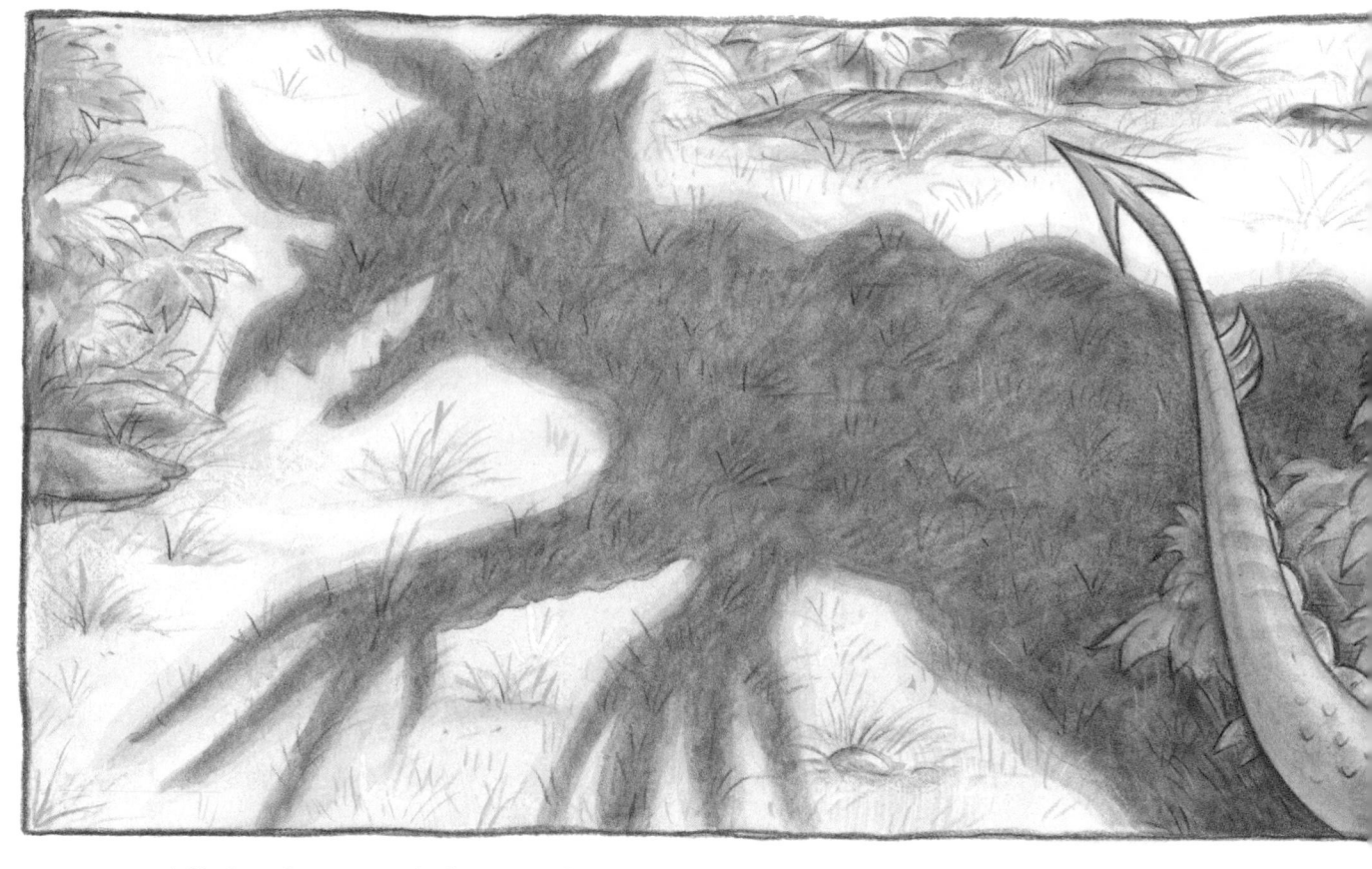

All the doors and shutters flew open. All the people in all of the town said, "SH-H-H-H! SH-H-H-H! SH-H-H-H!" Then all the shutters and doors slammed shut again.

Feeling sad and a little scared, Little Green Dragon went walking, walking, walking out of the town.

Then he went walking, walking, walking up the mountain to the castle. He went walking, walking, walking across the ribbledy, wobbledy stones of the courtyard. And up to the great stone steps.

Little Green Dragon drew a big, deep breath. "HI!" he shouted. "ANY-BODY HOME?"

All the windows and doors flew open. All the soldiers and footmen and maids and knights said, "SH-H-H-H!" Then all the windows and doors slammed shut again.

Feeling a little sadder and a little more scared, Little Green Dragon went walking, walking, walking out of the courtyard of the castle.

10

Now everything was dark and scary. Little Green Dragon tiptoed—ever so quietly. He kept his tail raised high, so it wouldn't scrape along the ground. He didn't want to make the tiniest noise.

All at once Little Green Dragon heard a R-R-R-O-O-W-W-R-R-R! A blast of fire and smoke swept right past him. The flames came so close, all the scales on that side of Little Green Dragon turned up.

Little Green Dragon looked up. And up. And up. And UP!

He was looking at an enormous monster. At first, Little Green Dragon couldn't figure it out. What in the world could that gigantic thing be?

"R-R-R-O-O-W-W-R-R-R!" There went another blast of fire and smoke. Suddenly, Little Green Dragon realized IT WAS A DRAGON!

"Hi," said Little Green Dragon.

Big Dragon said: "Who are you? What are you doing in my country?"

"Just visiting," said Little Green Dragon.

"Don't you know I burn everything with my fiery breath?" snorted Big Dragon.

11

"Is that why everyone is so frightened? And says sh-h-h?" asked Little Green Dragon.

"Of course, it is!" roared Big Dragon. "I frighten the whole world. R-R-R-O-O-W-W-R-R-R!"

"You mustn't do that," said Little Green Dragon.

"Says who?" said Big Dragon.

"Says me," said Little Green Dragon. "It's not nice to frighten people and burn up stuff."

"Just who do you think you are—talking to a dragon like that! Don't you know that with one blast of my fiery breath I could burn you right up to a tiny little ash?" said Big Dragon.

"Maybe so, but you won't," said Little Green Dragon, "because I won't let you."

"*You won't let me?*" Big Dragon pointed and sneered, "*YOU?*"

"*ME!*"

"And who in the world *are you*?" asked Big Dragon.

"I am the Little Green Dragon."

"You're *what*?" roared Big Dragon. And here came another blast of fiery breath. The scales on the other side of Little Green Dragon turned up.

"I'm a dragon. I'm the Little Green Dragon."

"You're a ... You're a ..."

"*I am a dragon!*"

"A dra ... a dra ... a drago ... a *dragon*?" Big Dragon gasped. He began to wheeze. And then he began to chortle. And then he began to snort. He laughed and he

12

laughed. He har-har-ed and he ho-ho-ed. The tears ran down his face and put out his fire. He laughed some more. And some more. Finally he fell down and rolled over on his back, still laughing. He waved his feet in the air. He thumped his big scaly tail on the ground.

Well, as you may know, dragons are just like water bugs and beetles and things like that. When they get on their backs, they can't get up. And that's the end of them.

Little Green Dragon knew this. And the Big Dragon knew this too. He stopped har-har-ing and ho-ho-ing. He stopped laughing at Little Green Dragon.

"Please help me, Little Green Dragon," Big Dragon said.

"Will you stop frightening people and going 'R-R-R-O-W-R'?"

"I promise," Big Dragon answered very solemnly without a single chuckle or fiery blast.

Just a tiny bit scared, Little Green Dragon went walking, walking, walking right up to Big Dragon.

He pushed—and he pushed! He pushed against the monster's scaly side. He was *so-o-o-o-o BIG*! Finally Big Dragon was on his feet again.

"Thank you, Little uh …. Well, I guess you *are* a dragon," Big Dragon said, oh, so softly and went sneaking off into the forest.

Little Green Dragon suddenly heard a great racket and roaring and cheering. He looked behind him. There was the lion who had laughed. And the woman who had laughed. And the people of the town and the soldiers and footmen and knights and ladies of the castle who had not laughed, because they had slammed all their doors and windows. Nobody was laughing and nobody was saying, "SH-H-H-H!" They were yelling and roaring: "Ya-a-ay, Little Green Dragon! You saved us from the big dragon! Yay, yay! Hooray!"

And from her window high in the castle, the princess waved and smiled.

"*I am* the dragon," said Little Green Dragon quietly.

14

Little Green Dragon Wants to Be Somebody Else

ONCE upon a long-ago morning, the Little Green Dragon woke up. He had slept on a purple velvet pillow at the foot of the big grand bed of the princess. Little Green Dragon loved the princess, because she was *so-o-o-o-o pretty* in so many ways.

Everyone loved the Little Green Dragon too, because of who he was.

Little Green Dragon took off his little green nightcap with the l-o-n-n-g tassel. He put on his little green daycap with the feather that curled. He made a face at the mirror. He wasn't happy. He was *so-o-o-o-o tired* of being the Little Green Dragon. He wanted to be Somebody Else.

Little Green Dragon saw *another* purple velvet pillow. On it sat the golden crown of the prince. It was beau-u-utiful! Little Green Dragon snatched off his little green daycap. He put the crown on his head. It fell down over his eyes and rested on his little, long green snout. But he felt *grand*!

Little Green Dragon went walking, walking, walking down the golden stairs. On he went—walking, walking, walking into the breakfast room.

When the princess saw the Little Green Dragon, she gasped, "Oh! Little Green Dragon, you mustn't wear the crown of the prince!"

S-l-o-w-l-y, Little Green Dragon took off the crown. "Just wanted to be Somebody Else," he said softly and sadly.

Little Green Dragon went walking, walking, walking out into the courtyard of the palace where the soldiers stayed.

He saw a *gorgeous* hat hanging on a post. It was the major general's own hat. It was royal blue velvet. And it had a long white plume that curled. Little Green Dragon's cap had only a little green feather that curled.

Hoo! Hoo! Little Green Dragon stuck the major general's helmet on his head. The plume swept the ground, almost. O-o-o-h-w-e-e-e! Little Green Dragon felt grand!

Little Green Dragon went walking, walking, walking, to look for the soldiers. He wanted to show them how very grand he was. He found the soldiers practicing with swords.

But when the major general saw the Little Green Dragon, she gasped! "Oh! Little Green Dragon," she said. "You shouldn't wear my hat! I'm the major general. You are just the Little Green Dragon."

"Just wanted to be Somebody Else, a little bit," answered Little Green Dragon. He took off the beautiful, royal blue velvet helmet and handed it to the major general.

The Little Green Dragon went s-l-o-w-l-y walking, walking, walking out of the palace gates and across the bridge over the moat. He decided to go to town. Maybe in town he could be Somebody Else. Somebody besides just the Little Green Dragon.

When Little Green Dragon got to town, m-m-m, m-m-m! He smelled something good. It was the delicious cinnamon buns and raisin bread baking in the bakery. The Little Green Dragon went walking, walking, walking over to the bakery. He went inside the doors which swung.

"Hi!" said Little Green Dragon. "Anybody home?"

There was no answer.

Little Green Dragon went walking to the back of the bakery shop where the huge ovens were. Nobody was there. However, on a hook on the wall, Little Green Dragon saw the baker's big, tall white cap. Little Green Dragon stuck it on his head.

"Ta tee, ta tum, ta tah!" Oh, it was fun! Little Green Dragon really felt silly. Just then the baker walked in.

When he saw Little Green Dragon, he gasped. "Oh! Little Green Dragon!" he said. "You mustn't wear my cap. I have to keep it clean, clean, clean to wear while I'm baking."

S-l-o-w-l-y, Little Green Dragon pulled the crisp white cap over the little horn-bumps on his head. He handed it to the baker.

"Just wanted to be Somebody Else, for a while," he said sadly.

Little Green Dragon went walking, walking, walking around the town. And he thought and he thought: Whose hat? Whose hat?

He went looking into the offices where people worked. He looked and he looked and he looked. Finally, he opened a big wooden door and looked inside. Right in front of him, he saw a rack for hats. And there, right on top of it, was the tall fuzzy hat of the lord mayor. That hat was the tallest, most beautiful, softly shining fuzzy hat anyone has ever seen!

Little Green Dragon put it on. The lord mayor wasn't a very big man. His hat was small. It stayed on top of Little Green Dragon's head. It did not fall down over his eyes and onto his long green snout.

Oh, Little Green Dragon felt *so-o-o-o-o tall*! He felt so grown-up! He felt so dignified! He was *so-o-o-o-o proud* of himself!

Then the lord mayor came stepping briskly into the room. When he saw Little Green Dragon, he gasped! "Oh, Little Green Dragon!" he said. "You have on my hat!"

"I know," said Little Green Dragon. "I wanted to be Somebody Else, for a while. I'm tired of being a plain-old, little green dragon."

"But you're OUR Little Green Dragon," said the lord mayor. "You're the Little Green Dragon we love so much!"

"W-e-l-l," said Little Green Dragon. And then he thought some more.

"But, Lord Mayor. Your Honor. Sir. I did want to be Somebody Else, for a while!

"I tried on the crown of the prince, and the princess was cross at me.

"I tried on the major general's helmet with the beautiful curling plume. But she was cross at me.

"I tried on the baker's hat, all tall and white. But he was cross at me.

"And now, I've put on your tall fuzzy hat. And you're cross at me!"

"Little Green Dragon," said the lord mayor, "you go on home. We have a surprise for you."

"W-e-l-l," said Little Green Dragon.

"Now go on home," said the lord mayor.

So, the Little Green Dragon went walking, walking, walking back to the throne room, where the prince and princess were busy running the kingdom.

Little Green Dragon curled up on his little purple pillow by the princess's throne to wait for the lord mayor.

Very soon a page stepped to the door and proclaimed in a loud voice, "THE LORD MAYOR!"

And then, in a smaller voice, "And the baker!"

And in a still smaller, but different voice, "And the major general!"

And then in a most, most respectful voice, "His Majesty, the PRINCE."

The prince stood up from his throne. He walked over to the Little Green Dragon.

The major general walked toward the Little Green Dragon.

The baker walked toward the Little Green Dragon.

And the lord mayor walked toward the Little Green Dragon.

The baker then put his cap over Little Green Dragon's head. And again, it fell down to his little, long green snout.

The major general put her plumed helmet on top of the baker's cap on top of Little Green Dragon's head.

The lord mayor put his tall fuzzy hat on top of the major general's helmet, on top of the baker's hat, on top of Little Green Dragon's head.

And finally, very carefully, because it was a sign of his royal powers, the prince set his golden crown on the very tip-top of them all.

"*There!*" they all said to Little Green Dragon. "Now, do you feel like all of us, rolled up in one? Do you feel like a major general and a baker? And a lord mayor and a prince? Do you feel like Somebody Else because you have on all those hats?"

"N-o-o," said Little Green Dragon. His voice was muffled, because he was having to talk through so many hats that hung down over his snout. "N-o-o, I don't feel like

20

Somebody Else. I feel like a very squashed little green dragon."

One by one they lifted off their hats. First went the prince's crown. And then the lord mayor's hat. And then the major general's helmet. And then the baker's cap. And there stood Little Green Dragon with nothing on his head at all, except two funny little horn-bumps that little green dragons always have.

Then the princess came walking up. "Oh, Little Green Dragon, we love you because you're YOU," she said. "And I have a surprise for you." She held out Little Green Dragon's daycap with the feather that curled. He put it on his head and pranced around the room.

My! He felt grand! My! He felt glorious! My! Oh my, oh my! HE WAS THE LITTLE GREEN DRAGON!

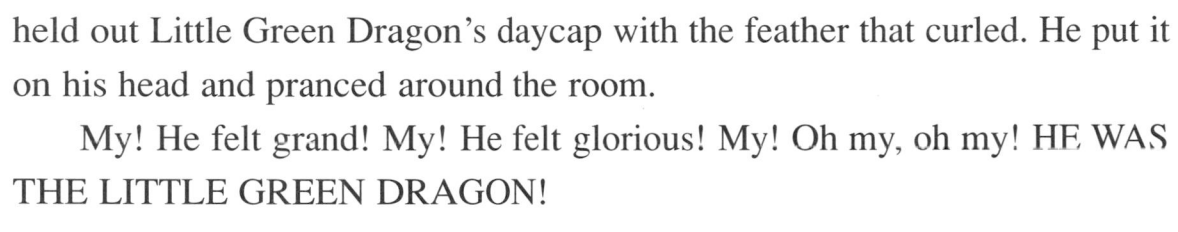

Where Do Little Green Dragons Come From?

ONCE upon a long-ago morning, the Little Green Dragon woke up. He took off his little green nightcap with the l-o-n-n-g tassel. He put on his little green daycap with the feather that curled. And all the time he was taking off his nightcap and putting on his daycap, he was wondering something. He was wondering where little green dragons came from. He had never seen another green dragon.

The Little Green Dragon lived in the castle with the princess and the prince.

This morning he went down the stairs to eat his breakfast. The cook was washing a plump green cabbage.

"Did I come from under a cabbage leaf?" asked Little Green Dragon.

"No-o-o," said the cook.

"I just—wondered," said Little Green Dragon. He went skippity, skippity, skippity out to the garden. The gardener was digging potatoes.

"Did I come out of the ground like a potato?" asked Little Green Dragon.

"No-o-o," said the gardener.

"I just—wondered," said Little Green Dragon.

Then the Little Green Dragon went skippity, skippity, skippity out to the barnyard. A big white goose had just laid a big white egg in a nest.

"Did I come out of an egg?" asked Little Green Dragon.

"No-o-o," hissed the goose.

"I just—wondered," said Little Green Dragon.

Then the Little Green Dragon went skippity, skippity, skippity back into the castle. And skippity, skippity, skippity into the throne room. The princess was sitting on her throne. Little Green Dragon loved the princess, and, yes, she was *so-o-o-o-o pretty*! The prince was sitting on his throne too. The court jester was hopping around acting funny, because that is what court jesters are supposed to do. The ladies and knights and the courtiers were all standing about. They all loved the Little Green Dragon—and who said he was *so-o-o-o-o ugly*?

"Hi!" said Little Green Dragon shyly. Then … "Hey, everybody, where did I come from?"

"God made you," said the princess, "just like God makes everyone and everything."

"But where did I come from?" asked Little Green Dragon again.

Then everybody turned their heads and looked around at everybody else.

"Where *do* little green dragons come from?" they all asked.

Everybody shook their heads at everybody. Nobody knew.

"Ta ta-a-a ta tum ... Where do little green dragons come from?" sang the court jester. He did a somersault.

But nobody knew, because little green dragons are little bits of magic. And nobody knows where magic comes from.

"Little Green Dragon," said the princess, "we love you just the same, because you are our very own magical Little Green Dragon and because you are YOU!"

Little Green Dragon Gets Something New

ONCE upon a long-ago morning, the Little Green Dragon woke up. He took off his little green nightcap with the l-o-n-n-g tassel.

The princess said, "Let me see that *thing*."

"What *thing*?" asked Little Green Dragon.

"That old, dirty, worn-out nightcap *thing*!" answered the princess.

V-e-r-r-ry slowly, the Little Green Dragon handed the princess his nightcap. He loved his nightcap, because it was *so-o-o-o old*!

The princess held up the nightcap by the tips of her fingers. She turned it this way and that way, and that way and this way. She even tugged on the tassel!

"Well!" said the princess. "We'll just have to get you a new nightcap."

"With a long tassel?" the Little Green Dragon asked in a quavery voice.

"With a long tassel," said the princess.

"I don't want one, because I love my old, little green nightcap," said Little Green Dragon.

The princess patted him on his bumpy, little green head. She said: "Never mind, Little Green Dragon. Put on your little green daycap, and we'll go to town."

Very sadly, the Little Green Dragon put on his little green daycap with the feather that curled.

"Hand me that *thing*!" the princess said.

"What *thing*?" asked Little Green Dragon.

"That old, dirty, worn-out, little green daycap *thing*," the princess answered.

V-e-r-r-ry slowly, the Little Green Dragon handed the princess his little green daycap with the feather that curled.

The princess held it up by the tips of her fingers. She turned it this way and that way, and that way and this way. She even pulled on the feather!

"We'll just have to get you a new, little green daycap," she said.

"But I love my old, little green daycap," said Little Green Dragon. "It is *so-o-o-o old*."

"Never mind," said the princess. "Put it on. We'll go to town and buy
some new clothes."

Very sadly, the Little Green Dragon put on his old, little green daycap.
He went thumpy, thumpy, thumpy down the castle steps with the princess.

Six beautiful horses were hitched to the princess's carriage in the castle
courtyard. The princess and the Little Green Dragon climbed into the
carriage. It went rattley-bump, rattley-bump across the cobblestones.
Then it went rumblety-thunk, rumblety-thunk across the moat.

Pretty soon they came to the hat shop in the town. The coachman
opened the door and bowed. The princess and the Little Green Dragon got
out. The shopkeeper came to the door. The princess and the Little Green
Dragon went in.

"Do you have a little green nightcap?" asked the princess.

"With a l-o-n-n-g tassel?" Little Green Dragon asked.

The shopkeeper shook her head. "A little green nightcap with a long tassel? Never heard of such a thing."

"Do you have a little green daycap?" asked the princess.

"With a feather that curls?" asked Little Green Dragon. "That you find in the forest just like I did?"

The shopkeeper shook her head. "I never heard of such a thing," she repeated.

The Little Green Dragon was *so-o-o-o happy*! The shopkeeper would never ever be able to find a feather, and he would get to keep his little *old* daycap!

But then the shopkeeper said: "I'll be delighted to have them made for Your Highness. One with a tassel like this." She scrunched up her nose. "And"—she glared at the Little Green Dragon—"with a feather that, uh, *curls*!"

The princess and the Little Green Dragon went back to the castle. The very next day a great big box arrived.

Inside the box were two fat satin pillows. On one satin pillow sat a little green nightcap with a l-o-n-n-g tassel. It was a beautiful, green silk nightcap. The tassel was shiny gold. On the other pillow sat a little green daycap. It was a beautiful, green velvet daycap. And the feather—that curled—was bright red!

To please the princess, Little Green Dragon wore the *new* little green nightcap with the long tassel. And he wore the *new* little green daycap with the red feather that curled.

Nobody knows, except you and me, that underneath he wore his own *real* little green nightcap with the l-o-n-n-g tassel, and his own *real*, little green daycap with the feather that curled. The Little Green Dragon loved them both, because they were *so-o-o-o old*!

Little Green Dragon Ends War

ONE morning, Little Green Dragon woke up. He took off his little green nightcap with the l-o-n-n-g tassel. He put on his little green daycap with the feather that curled. Then he went walking, walking, walking down the stairs to eat his breakfast.

Next, Little Green Dragon went to the throne room to see the princess. Oh, my! What a commotion was going on! Ladies-in-waiting and courtiers and pages were running around all over the place. The princess was sitting on a great big gold throne next to the prince. She looked *so-o-o-o worried*!

Little Green Dragon stepped up the three purple steps to the throne. "What's the matter?" he asked.

"The wicked king is coming to make war on us again," cried the princess.

"I'll help!" said Little Green Dragon, waving his prickly tail.

"Oh, Little Green Dragon," the princess said gently. "This is *war*!"

Just then, a whole troop of soldiers came clanking in.

The princess held up her hand. Everybody was quiet. "Wait!" she said.

"I am going to help!" Little Green Dragon shouted.

"Oh, Little Green Dragon," said the soldiers. "This is WAR!"

"I'm going to ask the wicked king not to make war," said Little Green Dragon. "I am!" And he did.

All by himself, the Little Green Dragon went marching, marching, marching up the mountains, down the valleys, across the plains to the country where the wicked king lived.

Finally, the Little Green Dragon could see the castle of the wicked king. The Little Green Dragon went marching, marching, marching up to the castle. Bam! Bam! Bam! He knocked on the castle door.

A great big soldier in a great big hat opened the door. "What do you want?" he asked.

"I've come to see the wicked king," said Little Green Dragon.

"He won't be scared of a tiny little dragon like you," said the soldier.

"I haven't come to scare him. I've come to talk to him," said Little Green Dragon.

The soldier took the Little Green Dragon to the throne room of the wicked king.

"What do you want?" roared the wicked king.

"I want to know why you are going to make war on the princess," said Little Green Dragon.

The wicked king sputtered and got very red in the face. "She took some of my land!" he roared.

So the Little Green Dragon went marching, marching, marching back to the princess.

"Oh, Little Green Dragon, I'm so glad to see you," cried the princess. "I've been *so-o-o-o worried*!"

"It's okay," said Little Green Dragon. He told the princess what the king had said about her taking some of his land.

"I didn't mean to take any of his land. I didn't know anyone owned that land," said the princess. "Tell him I'll give it back."

"Okay," said Little Green Dragon. And he went marching, marching, marching back to the wicked king's country.

"The princess says you can have your land back," announced Little Green Dragon to the wicked king.

"I never heard of such a thing," said the wicked king. "She's going to *give* the land back to me?"

"Yep," said Little Green Dragon.

"Why, why, why? I ... I don't ... I don't know what to do," sputtered the wicked king.

"Well, you can let her keep half of it," said Little Green Dragon.

"I'll do that very thing," said the *good* wicked king.

So the Little Green Dragon went marching, marching, marching back to the princess.

"The good wicked king says for you to keep half of the land. And he's not going to make war—not cver again," Little Green Dragon said proudly.

The princess clapped her hands and kissed the Little Green Dragon on his little, long green snout. All the people clapped their hands and cheered.

Little Green Dragon was so happy that he breathed fire! He curled up on his purple velvet pillow at the feet of the princess.

"My," he sighed. "She is *so-o-o-o pretty*!" And then he fell asleep.

Little Green Dragon Has an Adventure

ONCE upon a long-ago morning, the Little Green Dragon woke up. First, he opened his big green eyes. Then, he decided to have an *adventure*.

The Little Green Dragon went walking, walking, walking through the castle. He came to the throne room. The princess was sitting on the gold throne. He loved the princess, because she was *so-o-o-o good* to every single person.

Little Green Dragon said, "I've come to say good-bye for a little while."

"Where are you going, Little Green Dragon?" asked the princess. The princess loved the Little Green Dragon, because he was *so-o-o-o special*!

"I'm going to have an ADVENTURE!" announced Little Green Dragon.

The Little Green Dragon went walking, walking, walking out of the castle. He went walking, walking, walking over the ribbledy, wobbledy cobblestones of the castle courtyard.

"Where are you going, Little Green Dragon?" asked the soldiers.

"I'm going to have an ADVENTURE!" announced Little Green Dragon.

The Little Green Dragon went walking, walking, walking down the crinchy, crunchy rock road on the Other Side of the Mountain. The Other Side of the Mountain was the place to have an *adventure*.

The sky was blue. The grass was green. The Little Green Dragon went walking, walking, walking on the Other Side of the Mountain, looking for an adventure.

He saw a brownish speckled egg lying in the green grass. The egg looked cold and all alone.

"Hey!" called Little Green Dragon. "Who belongs to this egg?"

Nobody answered.

"Oh, dear," sighed Little Green Dragon. "I wanted to have an adventure. But somebody has gone off and left this egg. If I don't sit on it, it won't ever hatch."

Sadly, the Little Green Dragon sat down on the egg.

Three children, just about your size, came running by. They stopped.

"What are you?" the children asked.

"I'm the Little Green Dragon," answered Little Green Dragon.

"What are you doing?" asked the children.

"I'm sitting on an egg. Then I'm going to have an *adventure*."

"O-o-oh, Little Green Dragon," said the children, "you're *so-o-o-o-o silly*!" And they ran off, giggling.

The Little Green Dragon sat on the egg, and he sat on the egg. Pretty soon, a woman came by. She was carrying a basket of fruit and vegetables. She stopped.

"What are you?" asked the woman.

"I'm the Little Green Dragon," answered Little Green Dragon.

"What are you doing?" asked the woman.

"I'm sitting on an egg," said Little Green Dragon. "Then I'm going to have an *adventure*."

"O-o-oh, Little Green Dragon," said the woman, "you're *so-o-o-o-o silly*!" And she walked off, giggling.

The Little Green Dragon sat on the egg, and he sat on the egg. He wished the egg's mother would come back—then he could go on and have his adventure.

Pretty soon, a man came by leading a cow. The man stopped.

"What are you?" asked the man.

"I'm the Little Green Dragon," answered Little Green Dragon.

"What are you doing?" asked the man.

"I'm sitting on an egg," explained Little Green Dragon, tiredly. "Then I'm going to have an *adventure*."

"O-o-oh, Little Green Dragon," said the man, "you're *so-o-o-o-o silly*!"
And the man went off, giggling. His cow might have been giggling too.

The Little Green Dragon sat on the egg, and he sat on the egg. The sun
was hot in the bright blue sky. He wished he could go and have his adventure. The Little Green Dragon sat on the egg, and he sat on the egg. The sun
began to go down. And the Little Green Dragon got very hungry. Then he
heard something. It was just the tiniest little noise. V-e-r-r-ry carefully, the
Little Green Dragon got up off the egg. Sure enough, there was a little
crack in the egg!

The Little Green Dragon heard the tiniest little sound again. Something
was pecking against the inside of the egg!

The Little Green Dragon's big green eyes became even bigger. He
watched and watched. He watched some more.

Finally, with a wiggle and a bump, the egg cracked open. With a wiggle
and a bump, out stepped a little chick. It looked kind of squashed and
funny.

Ever so gently, the Little Green Dragon blew on the chick. Pretty soon,
the chick fluffed out. It was brown and yellow.

Ever so carefully, the Little Green Dragon picked up the little chick. Ever so gently, the Little Green Dragon went walking, walking, walking back up the crinchy, crunchy rock road on the Other Side of the Mountain. He went walking, walking, walking back across the ribbledy, wobbledy cobblestones.

The princess came running out to meet him.

"Oh! Little Green Dragon! Where have you been so long? We were all so worried!"

"I have had an ADVENTURE," announced the Little Green Dragon. "Look!" And he held out the chick for the princess to see.

And you know what? When that chick grew up, the Little Green Dragon found out it wasn't a chicken. And it wasn't a duck. And it wasn't a goose. And it wasn't a swan with a long beautiful neck. It was a guinea hen!

And how the Little Green Dragon loved it, because when people first saw it they thought it was *so-o-o-o-o ugly* too!

Little Green Dragon Wakes Up Feeling Mean

ONCE upon a long-ago morning, the Little Green Dragon woke up. He *yanked* off his little green nightcap with the l-o-n-n-g tassel. He *yanked* on his little green daycap with the feather that curled. In fact, he *yanked* it on so hard he pulled it right down over his eyes! He pushed it up from his eyes just a little bit and peered around. O-o-oh! He felt *so-o-o-o-o mean*!

Little Green Dragon kicked his beautiful, purple velvet pillow clear across the room.

Then Little Green Dragon went stomp, stamp, stomp, stamp down the stairs to eat his breakfast. My, he felt *mean*!

"Good morning, Little Green Dragon," said the cook.

"R-R-R-O-O-O-W-W-R-R-R!" said Little Green Dragon. A spurt of fire came out of his mouth and burned his own piece of toast. My! That made him feel even MEANER!

Little Green Dragon went stomp, stamp, stomp, stamp out the back door.

"Good morning, Little Green Dragon," said the gardener.

"R-R-R-O-O-O-W-W-R-R-R!" said the Little Green Dragon. And fire came out of his mouth.

"Hey!" said the gardener. "You burned my bean stalk."

My! Little Green Dragon felt MEAN!

Little Green Dragon went stomp, stamp, stomp, stamp all around the castle barnyard. He growled "R-R-R-O-O-O-W-W-R-R-R!" and breathed fire. The horses whinnied and danced around. He growled "R-R-R-O-O-W-

W-R-R-R!" and breathed fire. The chickens ran away. He growled "R-R-R-O-O-O-W-W-R-R-R!" and breathed fire. The cows moo-oo-ed.

My, he felt MEAN!!!

Little Green Dragon went stomp, stamp, stomp, stamp to the courtyard where the soldiers stayed.

"Good morning, Little Green Dragon!" yelled the soldiers.

"R-R-R-O-O-O-W-W-R-R-R!" growled the Little Green Dragon. Fire came out of his mouth.

The soldiers all stood and stared. The Little Green Dragon went stomp, stamp, stomp, stamp across the moat. He went stomp, stamp, stomp, stamp down the side of the mountain until he came to the town. The people in the town were all walking around being busy.

"Good morning, Little Green Dragon," called the people.

"R-R-R-O-O-O-W-W-R-R-R!!" growled the Little Green Dragon. A flame came out of his mouth. It curled the shingle on one of the houses. My! He felt MEAN!

The people of the town went running about saying, "What ever is the matter with the Little Green Dragon?" Some of them ran up the mountain to tell the princess.

Pretty soon, here came the purple carriage with the golden crown on top. Six horses pulled the carriage of the princess.

"LITTLE GREEN DRAGON!" called the princess.

"R-R-R-O-O-O-W-W-R-R-R!" growled the Little Green Dragon.

"Whatever is the matter with you?" asked the princess. "You growled at the cook and burned the toast. You growled at the gardener and burned the bean stalk. You frightened the horses and chickens and cows. You growled at the soldiers. You growled at the people and burned the shingle. Whatever has happened to our own Little Green Dragon?"

"R-r-r-o-o-o-w-w-r-r-r !" mumbled the Little Green Dragon.

"When you're feeling better," said the princess, "I want you to tell everybody you are sorry. Right now, you get in the carriage and come home with me."

The Little Green Dragon rode in the corner of the carriage. Every time he breathed, a little puff of fire came out. Now he didn't feel mean. He felt very lonesome.

The carriage returned to the castle. The Little Green Dragon stepped out. The courtiers helped the princess out.

The princess walked into the throne room. The Little Green Dragon came walking, walking, walking behind the princess. He wasn't going stomp, stamp, stomp, stamp any more. He wasn't breathing flames, just a little trickle of smoke.

The princess sat down on the throne.

The Little Green Dragon sat in front of her.

"Well, Little Green Dragon!" said the princess, "I guess you can be a big scary dragon if you want to. You can breathe out fire. You can be meaner and meaner. And everybody will run away. Do you want to be a big MEAN green dragon?"

"And everybody will run away from me and be scared?" asked the Little Green Dragon.

"Yes, they will," answered the princess.

"I don't think I'll be a big mean dragon," said Little Green Dragon. "I'd be *so-o-o-o-o lonesome*."

The Little Green Dragon went walking past the fireplace on his way to tell everybody he was sorry. He went "R-R-R-O-O-O-W-W-R-R-R!" one more time, just to see if he could light the logs in the fireplace with his fiery breath.

Nope. No flame came out of his mouth. You have to be feeling very mean to breathe out *that* kind of fire. And the Little Green Dragon wasn't feeling mean anymore. He was feeling just like a plain, little green dragon.

But later on, Little Green Dragon tried lighting birthday cake candles and roasting marshmallows with his fiery breath—just practicing.

Yep. He still had his own Little Green Dragon fire.

Little Green Dragon Goes Out Into the Night

ONCE upon a time one night the Little Green Dragon woke up. Yes, that's right. It was the middle of the night. The Little Green Dragon had never been awake at night before. The princess always put him to bed when the red sun was just going down behind the lavender mountains.

O-o-oh, it was dark! It was *so-o-o-o-o dark*, the bed where the princess was sleeping looked like a big black hill. He couldn't even see the princess!

The Little Green Dragon looked at his own little green self. He wasn't green any more! Where did his color go?

The Little Green Dragon put a little green paw up to his little green head. Yep, he still had on his little green nightcap with the long gold tassel. He peered at the long gold tassel. He could barely see it. And it wasn't gold any more! It was just gray.

The Little Green Dragon decided to get up. He wanted to see what the rest of the world looked like at night.

He decided not to put on his little green daycap with the feather that curled. That was his *day*cap. This was night. He left on his little green night-cap with the l-o-n-n-g tassel.

The Little Green Dragon went tippy, tippy, tippy, tippy down the stairs. There wasn't a sound. The whole world was sleeping.

The Little Green Dragon went tippy, tippy, tippy, tippy through the castle. There wasn't a sound. The whole world was sleeping.

The Little Green Dragon went tippy, tippy, tippy, tippy through the kitchen. There wasn't a sound. The cook was sleeping. The whole world was sleeping.

The Little Green Dragon went tippy, tippy, tippy, tippy through the door. There wasn't a sound. The guards were sleeping. The whole world was sleeping.

Now the Little Green Dragon was outside. He peered a-l-l-l-l around. *What was that sound?* He jumped. The world outside was *not* sleeping! The Little Green Dragon could hear all kinds of little scritches and creaks and rustles and scratches. The daytime world was sleeping. The nighttime world was awake.

"Hooooo, hooooo!"

The Little Green Dragon jumped even higher! Whatever in the world was that?

"I am a brave Little Green Dragon," he muttered to himself. He wanted to run, run, run back under the bed. Instead, he went tippy, tippy, tippy, tippy on into the garden.

"Crench, crench, crench."

The Little Green Dragon jumped! What was that? "I am a brave Little Green Dragon," he muttered to himself. He peered about.

All the colors were gone! The flowers weren't red and yellow anymore! They were just different shades of gray. The grass wasn't green anymore. It was dark gray. The trees didn't have brown bark and green leaves anymore. They had black bark and black leaves. And something was still going "Crench, crench, crench!" And something was still going "Hooo, hoooo!"

"I am a brave Little Green Dragon," he muttered to himself. He peered around some more, v-e-r-r-ry slowly. Ho! The Little Green Dragon could see what was making that crench noise. Something like a rabbit was eating something like a cabbage. It didn't look like a real rabbit. And it didn't look like a real cabbage. The rabbit wasn't a nice, soft brown rabbit color. It was just a dark gray shape of a rabbit. And the cabbage wasn't that soft, green cabbage color. It was just a dark gray shape of a cabbage.

Hmmmmm, thought the Little Green Dragon, nighttime is very strange.

"Hooo, hooo!"

The Little Green Dragon jumped higher than ever! "I am a brave Little Green Dragon," he muttered to himself. V-e-r-r-ry slowly, he lifted his head to see what was making that strange scary noise. He saw something. The something had eyes that shone in the dark. The something looked like a bird. Just a dark shape of a bird.

Not much of a bird, thought the Little Green Dragon, not like all the happy, chirpy, fluttery day birds.

The Little Green Dragon was thinking he didn't like the dark very much. He was wondering where all the colors had gone. He looked up even farther to see what happened to the blue, blue sky at night. When the Little Green Dragon saw the sky, he gasped.

"Oh! Oh! Oh! I must tell the princess," the Little Green Dragon cried.

The Little Green Dragon went running, running, running back up the garden path.

The Little Green Dragon went running, running, running through the door and back across the kitchen.

The Little Green Dragon went running, running, running back up the stairs.

The Little Green Dragon went running, running, running—BUMP!—against the princess's bed!

"Wake up! Wake up!" the Little Green Dragon shouted. "Wake up! Wake up! Something strange and wonderful has happened!"

"What's the matter, Little Green Dragon?" mumbled the princess, very sleepily.

"Oh, Princess, you have to get up; you have to get up. Come and see!"

"*What*, Little Green Dragon?"

"Come and see! The sky is full of holes! That's very bad. But heaven is shining right through those holes! And that's very good," shouted the Little Green Dragon.

"Oh-h-h, Little Green Dragon," the princess said gently. "The sky isn't full of holes. Those are stars you see."

The princess patted the Little Green Dragon on the head. "Little Green Dragon," she explained, "stars are little worlds, far, far, far away from our world. The stars shine at night. Now you go back to bed and go to sleep."

"Okay," said the Little Green Dragon. He went back and lay down on his purple velvet pillow which didn't look purple anymore. He thought about the night. He thought about the stars.

Just as the Little Green Dragon was going back to sleep, he whispered: "Well, maybe there aren't any holes in the sky. Maybe the princess is right. But I still think heaven shines through at night, when the whole world is sleeping."

And the Little Green Dragon fell asleep too.

Little Green Dragon Wants to Be a Hero

ONCE upon a long-ago morning, the Little Green Dragon woke up. But before he even opened his big green eyes, he said to himself, "Today I want to be a HERO!"

Very quickly, he jumped up. He snatched off his little green nightcap with the l-o-n-n-g tassel. He yanked on his little green daycap with the feather that curled.

The Little Green Dragon went into the kitchen. And, sure enough, he had a chance to be a hero right off. A big fire was blazing in the kitchen stove. The Little Green Dragon went running, running, running. He grabbed a pail of water, threw it on the fire, and put it out. "There!" he said proudly to the cook.

"What do you mean, 'there'?" asked the cook crossly. "I just got the fire started for breakfast, and now you've thrown water all over it."

"I was just trying to be a hero," sighed Little Green Dragon.

He went out into the courtyard and—oh my! The minute he stepped outside he had a chance to be a hero, right off. He saw two knights riding at each other with their lances. He had to do something, quick.

So, the Little Green Dragon went running in between the two horses. He breathed out fire and smoke with all his might.

51

The two horses reared up! The knights fell onto the ground with a clatter of armor—and a lot of yelling.

"There!" said Little Green Dragon.

"What do you mean, 'there'?" yelled the knights. "You made the horses throw us onto the ground!"

"But I was afraid you were going to hurt yourselves," explained the Little Green Dragon.

"We were only practicing," said the knights.

"I was just trying to be a hero," sighed Little Green Dragon sadly.

While the soldiers were still fussing, the Little Green Dragon suddenly dashed off. A man was leaning over the wall around the moat. The man was twisting around in a very strange manner. He was about to fall in!

The Little Green Dragon went running, running, running! He flew through the air in a great tackle! He grabbed the man around the legs and knocked him back away from the moat.

The man hit the ground, hard.

"Why did you do that?" he shouted.

"I was trying to save you," answered Little Green Dragon.

"Save me? Save me?" sputtered the man. "Didn't you see my fishing pole? I finally caught the big trout that lives in the moat!"

"No-o-o," answered Little Green Dragon sadly. "I was just trying to be a hero."

BUT, at that moment, the man and the soldiers stopped fussing.

Everybody stopped what they were doing. Everybody listened. A voice was calling, "Help! Help!"

It was the princess!

Faster than anyone, the Little Green Dragon, who really was *so-o-o-o-o brave*, went running into the castle.

The Little Green Dragon could hear the princess calling from the throne room. "Fire! The throne room is filled with smoke! Help!"

The Little Green Dragon went running, running, running into the throne room. He went running straight to the princess. He took her by the hand and led her outside.

Then he clanged the great bell that hung in the courtyard. "FIRE!" he yelled. Everybody came running to put out the fire.

"Oh, Little Green Dragon!" said the princess. "You saved me from the fire and smoke. You're a HERO!"

And the men and the soldiers shouted, "Yea! Yea! Little Green Dragon, you're a HERO!"

"I am not a hero," answered Little Green Dragon quietly. "I just did what I had to do—but maybe that *is* what a hero really does."

LEARNING FROM THE LITTLE GREEN DRAGON

The Little Green Dragon's adventures provide parents and teachers with perfect opportunities to explore ideas about life, outlooks, and behavior with children. The following guide gives a lesson suggestion and set of questions for each of the ten stories. The purpose of the lessons and questions is twofold: first, to encourage discussion between children and adults about actions and events in the stories; second, to encourage children to apply the ideas and issues to their own lives, families, and friends. These lessons and questions represent important morals and concepts of the stories, but others certainly are possible. The Little Green Dragon would be *so-o-o-o-o pleased* with all the ways that readers find his adventures to be helpful.

Little Green Dragon Meets the Princess

Lesson:
People should be judged by more than appearances. We must take time
to see and know people as they really are.

Exploring the Adventure:
1. How does everyone at first judge the Little Green Dragon?
    Why might they react as they do?
2. Do you agree with them?
3. What do the people and the princess learn about the Little Green Dragon?
4. How does the Little Green Dragon at first judge the princess?
    (Why does he say he loves her?)
5. What does the Little Green Dragon learn about the princess?

Little Green Dragon Meets Big Dragon

Lesson:
Always remember your own sense of self-worth. Be true to yourself and
your values and recognize your abilities.

Exploring the Adventure:
1. Why is the Little Green Dragon laughed at and ridiculed?
2. What does the Little Green Dragon know about himself?
3. What reason does the Little Green Dragon give the Big Dragon for
    not frightening people? What does this tell you about the Little Green
    Dragon?
4. What does the Little Green Dragon show about himself when he stands
    up to the Big Dragon? What do you think about the Little Green
    Dragon's actions?

5. Why do you think the Little Green Dragon helped the Big Dragon?
   Would you have done the same?

Little Green Dragon Wants to Be Somebody Else

Lesson:
Be yourself. True contentment and peace come from within, not from without.

Exploring the Adventure:
1. Why do you think the Little Green Dragon likes wearing the different hats?
2. If the Little Green Dragon could keep one hat, would it really make him Somebody Else?
3. How does the Little Green Dragon feel when he is wearing all the hats?
4. Why, according to the lord mayor and the princess, is the Little Green Dragon truly loved?
5. Do you ever feel as if you want to be Somebody Else? Why?

Where Do Little Green Dragons Come From?

Lesson:
God is the source of all that is.

Exploring the Adventure:
1. Who, says the princess, made the Little Green Dragon and "everyone and everything"?
2. Does the Little Green Dragon seem to agree with that?
3. Why might the Little Green Dragon wonder exactly where he came from? Why would this be important to him?
4. Where do you think magic comes from?
5. Are magic and imagination the same? Explain.

Little Green Dragon Gets Something New

Lesson:
Be sure to consider the wishes and feelings of those you are helping.
Also, remember to be kind to those who are helping you.

Exploring the Adventure:
1. The princess is trying to be nice in buying new caps for the Little Green Dragon, but what is she forgetting?
2. How does this make the Little Green Dragon feel?
3. Do you have favorite clothes that you can't imagine giving up? How does wearing them make you feel?
4. Can you understand, then, why the Little Green Dragon wants to keep his old caps?

5. Do you think the Little Green Dragon should wear the new caps for the princess? Why or why not?

Little Green Dragon Ends War

Lesson:

When there are disagreements, try to settle them peacefully.

Exploring the Adventure:

1. How does the kingdom at first prepare for war?
2. What is the Little Green Dragon's method of preventing a war?
3. What do you think caused the misunderstanding between the wicked king and the princess?
4. Is the wicked king really wicked? How do you know?
5. What is your opinion of the Little Green Dragon and his actions in this adventure?

Little Green Dragon Has an Adventure

Lesson:

Helping and loving others are among life's most rewarding adventures.

Exploring the Adventure:

1. What kind of adventure do you think the Little Green Dragon wants to have?
2. What does sitting on the egg show about the Little Green Dragon's character?
3. Why do you think the Little Green Dragon isn't bothered by people calling him silly?
4. Does the Little Green Dragon seem satisfied with his adventure? Why or why not?
5. How is your life an adventure?

Little Green Dragon Wakes Up Feeling Mean

Lesson:

Being mean to others can hurt yourself too.

Exploring the Adventure:

1. Do you ever wake up feeling mean? Why do you think this happens?
2. Why might the Little Green Dragon feel mean?
3. How does the princess react to the Little Green Dragon's meanness? Does this help him?
4. Why does the Little Green Dragon begin feeling lonesome?

Who brings about his loneliness?

5. Do you ever feel lonely after acting on feelings of meanness or anger?

Little Green Dragon Goes Out Into the Night

Lesson:

Heaven shines through wherever we see it in life.

Exploring the Adventure:

1. Do new, different, or strange surroundings ever frighten you?
2. Why does the Little Green Dragon keep reminding himself that he is brave?
3. What does the Little Green Dragon find good about "holes in the sky"?
4. How can you be like the Little Green Dragon in a new or strange place?
5. What does this adventure tell you about curiosity and imagination?

Little Green Dragon Wants to Be a Hero

Lesson:

True heroes react from the heart and do what has to be done.

Exploring the Adventure:

1. How has the Little Green Dragon already proven himself to be a hero in other adventures?
2. What happens when the Little Green Dragon *tries* to be a hero?
3. What happens when he reacts from the heart to a real danger?
4. What is the Little Green Dragon's definition of a hero?
5. How have you been a hero today?

About the Author

Mari Privette Ulmer is a professional author and attorney who lives in Ranchos de Taos, New Mexico. She is the author of *Sign Here*, a book of contract law for consumers, as well as many articles and stories for periodicals. She is also a mystery writer and a member of Southwest Writers.

A native of Kansas City, Missouri, Mari began telling stories as a young girl baby-sitting neighborhood children. She later worked as a television "Story Lady in the Book" at KCMO in Kansas City before entering law school. She graduated in 1962 from the University of Missouri at Kansas City, where she was editor-in-chief of the *Law Review* and was named the outstanding woman law student in the state. She worked for a Kansas City law firm before moving to New Mexico. She has two children and four grandchildren and is active in the Catholic church.

About the Artist

Mary Kurnick Maass, an illustrator and graphic artist, received the 1990 Magazine Merit Award for illustration from the Society of Children's Book Writers. She is a graduate of Columbus College of Art & Design in Columbus, Ohio. Her client list includes many companies and publications.

Printed in the U.S.A.

20-2003-15M-1-99